Rivetina:

The Hardcore Wish Granting Fairy

Written and Illustrated by:
a.d.j.

PUBLISHING, LLC

Rivetina: The Hardcore Wish Granting Fairy

SDC Publishing, LLC

ISBN: 978-1-0878-0005-9

Published and printed in the United States of America

Dedication:

This book is dedicated to my grandpas:

Pap Jones,
Grandpa Van Gilder,
Pap Ozzie
&
Grandpa Willis

I love you.
Thank you for caring about the type of person that I would become.

Gratitude:

To my family who continues to support my wild imagination: Dad, Mom, Noel, Charity, and Grandma Jones.

* An extra thank you to my furry shadows: Lady and Buffy. In Memory of Lulabell (2018) & Little Mr. and Molly who went to heaven during the making of this book. (2019)

To my two writing buddies:

Michaela Hardy: Your sense of design is so much fun and your research invaluable.

Kimberly Matthews: Congratulations on your recent wedding. You and Simon are such a strong couple. We are going to change the world for the better.

To countless other friends: thank you all for your kindness.

The town of Hamilton is small and quiet.

It has pretty much everything that most towns do.

However, one thing that Hamilton seems to have a lot of . . .

are dreamers.

When Christina Smith was a young girl she loved fairies.

Although magical powers and changing the seasons were fun, it was the helpful fairies that she liked best.

You see, Tina Smith enjoyed fixing things and helping people.

As Tina got a little older she began to wonder about what type of job she should do. She felt that it would be a good idea to ask her Pap for some advice. So, late one summer morning, she walked up to her grandparents' house and asked him. He pointed to the old wooden porch swing, and they both sat down.

"Well, Tina girl, what's on your mind?" asked Pap Smith.
"Pap, I just don't know what I'm supposed to do with my life," she began. "Some of my friends are talking about what they want to do when they grow up. But I just don't know. I like fairies, but there aren't many of those in the world, and I like to help people, but in lots of different ways. How am I gonna figure this out?"

"Well Tina, honestly, I'm not quite so much worried about what you do, as to how you turn out," replied Pap Smith.
"Huh?" Tina's face twisted into a corn maze of questions.
"Keep your heart clean and your head straight, Tina girl. Whatever you do, or wherever you go, remember that. I want to know that you remember how to care about doing the right thing, and about what happens to other people," he finished.

Tina never forgot that conversation.

The years flew by, and one day Tina found herself fixing her neighbor's lawn mower by the back patio. Her feline pals, or 'furry shadows' as she liked to call them, were supervising the whole event.

Well, sort of.

Stan was sitting in his favorite wicker chair, while Mozzy sunbathed with all fours up in the air. None of the local birds were worried. It had been years since Stan felt the urge to chase any of them, and Mozzy usually let things go after she grabbed them.

As Tina finished with the last screw, the Henderson twins came bouncing around the corner of the house.
"Hi Miss Tina!" they chanted in unison.
"We have a problem, and wondered if you could help us," Anthony started. "It's about our ducks and their house," Amy finished.
"Your ducks, huh?" Tina said. "Ok, sure. I've been meaning to get the word around town that I'm available to do handiwork for people. You two can be my first official clients," she winked at them.
"Yay!" they squealed.

Tina stopped by her work shed to grab her larger tool box, and something else as well. The kids were both surprised and delighted.

"What do you have on your back?" asked Amy.
Tina smiled and explained. "Anthony, do you remember last week when you told me that you wanted to be a dinosaur when you grow up?"
The boy nodded.

"Well, when I was a kid, I really wanted to be a fairy. So I just decided to go ahead and make myself some wings."
"But they're scratchy!" exclaimed Amy as she touched one.
"Yeah, why are they like that?!" her brother asked.

"Because sandpaper is used to smooth over rough things, and I want people to know when I'm coming that I'm going to take their tough problems and smooth them over. I'm going to fix it," Tina replied. "I think I need a new name to go with my fairy identity." She cocked her head like a coonhound and gazed back into her work shed. After scanning around she spotted some metal laying against the wall.

"Hmmm, nuts . . . . bolts . . . . rivets . . . . I know! From now on my name is Rivetina, and I'm a hardcore wish granting fairy! I'll get the job done!"
The twins smiled at each other and followed her down the street.

When the trio arrived at the children's home they took Rivet-ina to the backyard. The Hendersons had a very pretty view of a small creek behind their home. This was the duck's play-ground. The land dropped off rather steeply from the house toward the creek, and there wasn't much room for a 'house' of any kind for the ducks.

"So, what do we need here?" Rivetina asked as she surveyed the yard.
"Well, every time it floods, the ducks don't really have any-where to go." Anthony pointed to the deck on the back of their house.
"We have a small dog house for them, but it's kind of in the way of us using the deck for other things," fretted Amy. "We don't know what to do."

Mrs. Henderson, popped her head out of the sliding glass door and waved at them. "Hey there, Tina. Thank you so much for stopping by. Earl and I thought that the kids had a great idea in asking you for some thoughts on our little duck issue. We really don't want to get rid of them; Anthony and Amy are so attached. We'll be happy to pay you for the work."

"You're very welcome, Mrs. Henderson; thank you for thinking of me. I've been trying to get my little handy business off the ground. Don't worry about the ducks. We'll get something nice put together for them," Rivetina called back.

Rivetina looked at the steep hill, and then she looked down at the creek. Her eyes lit up like fireflies in June.

"Hey, I know! The ducks don't need to get away from the creek, they just need a way to stay above the floodwaters!" Rivetina began. "We need to 'pull a Noah,' and build them an ARK!"

"What!?" the twins gasped.
"Hang on! I'm going to go grab my chainsaw, and some other supplies and tools. This is gonna be fun!"

Rivetina got to work sawing and hammering the boards and then added a waterproof sealant along the bottom of the new duck home. Finally, she tied airplane cables around four very sturdy trees along the creek and attached the ends to the corners of the little house boat. It bobbled up and down in the water, calmly.

Rivetina smiled and waved her hand towards the 'ark'.
"Henderson family, consider your wish granted!"
The entire family was now staring in awe at the quaint little invention.
"It has a raised interior and insulated walls so that the ducks can simply walk up into a safe dry spot, and the cables hang loose so that it will rise and fall with the water levels," she stated.

"Wow," they responded.
The Henderson family and their ducks were thrilled.

While she was cleaning up her tools, Mr. Bolero stopped by to chat with Mrs. Henderson. She pointed to the new avian ark and smiled. Mr. Bolero took off his blue ball cap, scratched his head, and grinned wider than a Tyrannosaurus Rex. "Well now, that is something!" he mused. "I don't suppose that you would have any ideas for a problem that I've got would you?" "I'd be happy to take a look," Rivetina smiled. "What's the issue?"

"Come on over to the local schools' camp site. I'd like you to see what you can do about some fire rings and my truck." Her stare was both amused and confused. "Oh, um ok." Upon reaching the camp site, Mr. Bolero gestured towards a pile of fire rings sitting in the dirt, and then back at his truck. He knelt down in the midst of the piles of rings and grinned. "Ta-da!" he chuckled.

"Every time the local school board plans outdoor activities for the kids, they change where they want stuff moved all around this area. These fire rings are for little quickie fire pits that we put up so that the kids can roast some s'mores or hotdogs. They just love it. The problem is that these rascals are sort of cumbersome to move, and it takes a while with a few people to load and unload them. Got any ideas?" Rivetina glanced at the pile of rings and then back at the truck. Suddenly, her eyes glowed like the Aurora Borealis. "Hey! What if they had wheels!? And you could attach them to your tail hitch!?" It was Mr. Bolero's turn to freeze and stare.

"Don't worry, Mr. Bolero! This is going to be great!" Rivetina stated as she turned to head for home. "I just need to stop at the hardware store to get some things and then pick up my welder from home." She took off like a derby horse.

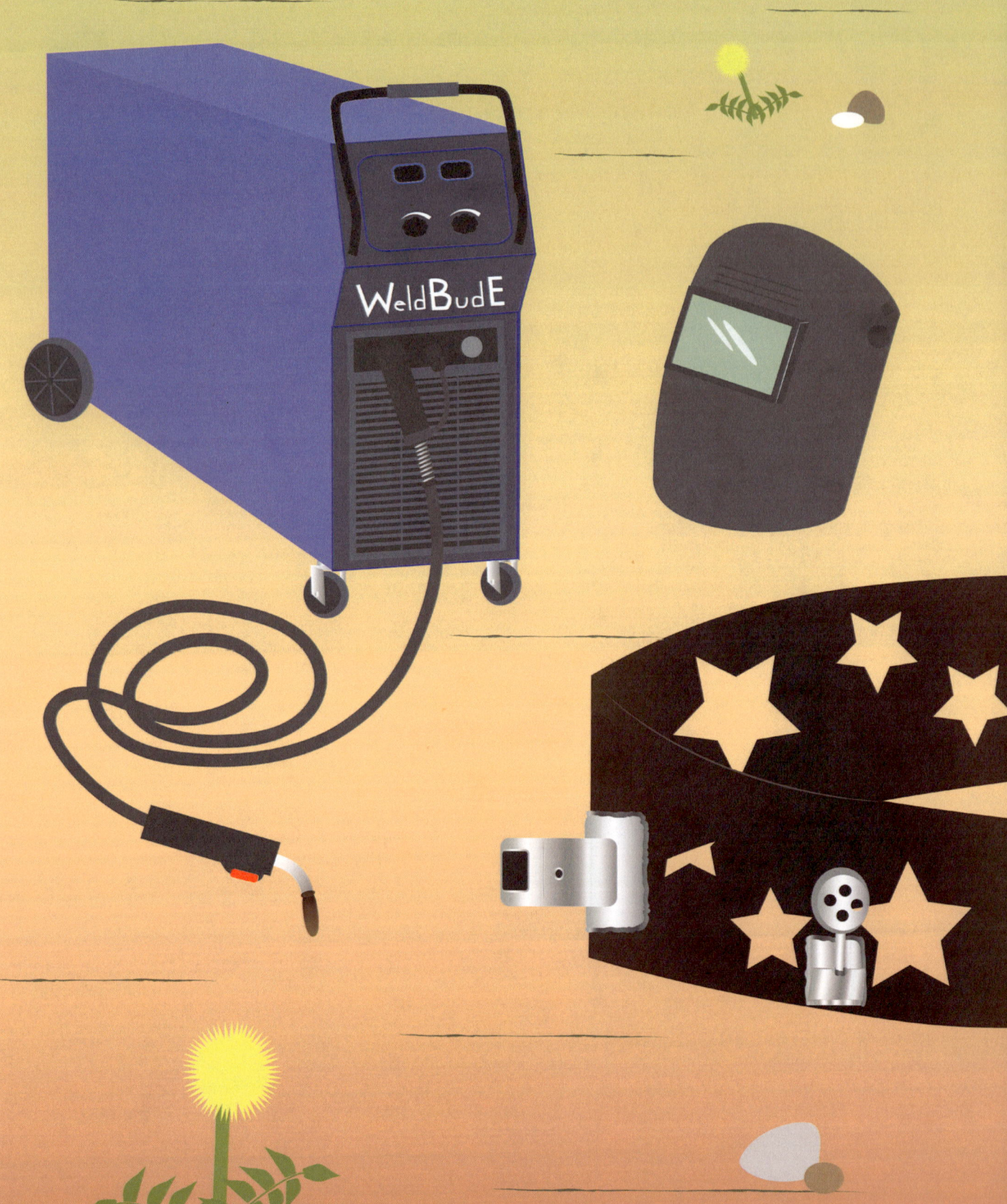

As soon as she had all of her gear, Rivetina put her welding mask and gloves on and went to work. She made sure that each ring had an attachment for a truck tail hitch, and then began adding wheels with sets of hinges. Within a few hours, she gave Mr. Bolero a phone call and asked him to take a look. He was thrilled.

"You see, with the attachment on each of these for your tail hitch, you can just latch it onto your truck and roll it to wherever you like. The hinges on the wheels allow you to fold them up while they are sitting on the ground for activities. That should keep the fire in the pit. You can just put them down when you need to move the pit. The wheels are metal, too, so you don't have to worry about any rubber melting."

She finished with a wave of her hand. "Mr. Bolero, consider your wish granted!"

He reached out and shook her hand several times. "I have never seen anything like this before. I can't believe that somebody didn't think of it sooner. We'll make sure to get your check this coming Monday. The board members are going fall out of their chairs when I show them these."

The next morning, while Rivetina was drinking her tea, the Henderson twins came knocking again. They plopped down on the large rug in the kitchen and began giving Stan and Mozzy belly rubs.

"How are you two this morning? Did your ducks settle in?" She asked.
"Oh, they're great," the kids chimed in unison.
"It's just that, we have another idea," began Anthony.
Rivetina set her cup down. "Ok, let's hear it."

Amy stopped petting Mozzy's belly and placed her hands on her knees. "Do you know Mrs. Chen? She's this really nice old lady that gives us music lessons. She has some kind of problem with water in her yard and stuff. Can you come take a look?"
"She's kind of worried about prices of things; that's why she hasn't called anybody else yet," Anthony added.

"I certainly do know her. She was my music teacher, too, a few years ago," Rivetina responded. With that said, she and the children set off for Mrs. Chen's little brick house.

Upon arrival, Rivetina began to dig in some wet areas and discovered some old water pipes that had begun to wear through. The holes were really starting to get large, and she realized that it needed taken care of immediately. Mrs. Chen was probably going to lose all of her water before the day was over if something wasn't done. As Rivetina surveyed the zig-zag of pipe issues in Mrs. Chen's yard, her frown gave in to gravity's pull.

"This is pretty bad," she thought. "I know how to fix this, but it's going to cost over $2,000 even before I add my labor to it."
At that moment, Mrs. Chen stepped outside.
"Hi there Mrs. Chen! Do you remember me?" Rivetina asked.
"Oh, of course I do. You were that stubborn little girl who just didn't know when to quit with the piano," Mrs. Chen grinned.
"Yes, that's me, ma'am." Rivetina smiled and then waved towards the splotchy mess.
Mrs. Chen slowly walked over to join her analyzing the scene. "Would you be able to fix this for me, dear? And if so, how much do you think that it will be?"

Rivetina put her hand on Mrs. Chen's shoulder and smiled. "Oh, don't worry, this won't be a problem at all. I just need to pick up some new pipe from the hardware store, and it'll be fixed in no time. I'll even put some pretty garden stones over it when I'm done so that you know exactly where this is if you ever need someone to find it in the future. I've got some of those at home that I painted bright colors last fall with a few of my kid friends. We just couldn't figure out where we wanted to put them. I guess now I know!"
As Rivetina turned to pick up her old red toolbox, she gave Mrs. Chen a reassuring grin. "As far as the cost. You will only be set back by about $1,500. That will take care of it."
"Oh, good! Thank you, Tina." Mrs. Chen was very relieved.

Need a Graphic Designer?
Yours Truly has what you're looking for. Check out my website: @
mhardystudios.com

Michaela Hardy at your service!

Hamilton Public Library

Presents:

Visiting Author:

Kimberly Matthews

Dust

This Saturday
in the Violet Lounge

@ 1 pm.

Tea and Scones will be
served following the reading.

Lost Angus Bull!
Last seen on Conners Road.
Call Steve McGill @
809-234-8902

Help Needed:

Household chores,
grocery and
errands,
rides for
appointments

Contact Donna:

390-872-0000

Goats for Sale:

Dairy and Brush
call Henry @

777-350-4001
777-350-4001
777-350-
777-350-4001
777-350-4001
777-350-4001

Hay for Sale:
Call Pete Jacobs:
903-107-4329

Looking to buy
used car parts:

Call Dave:
997-698-3245

I want to buy some
egg laying chickens.
Prefer Rhode Island
Reds.
Hattie Dently:
890-778-2344

Primo
Nails 2inch

Primo
Nails 2inch

Primo
Nails 2inch

Primo
Nails 2inch

Primo
Nails 2inch

Primo
Screws 90 pack

Primo
Screws 90 pack

Mr. Greenly's hardware store found its number one customer loading up her arms as usual late that morning. Rivetina was in such a hurry that she almost backed into the community bulletin board. As she left the register, Mr. Greenly pulled a handkerchief out of his red vest and blew his nose.

"Boy that sawdust works on my honker!" he laughed. So what's the project today?"
"Ah, just helping Mrs. Chen with a little water pipe situation. That's all," replied Rivetina.

Mr. Greenly's eyebrows launched for orbit. "Really? I know that she's been putting that off for a little while. Can she afford it?"

Rivetina glanced back over her shoulder at him. "Don't worry, Ted; she's going to be just fine." She then carried her load outside and dumped all of it into the bed of her truck. At that moment, Mr. Wimble the town mayor, and Mrs. Greenly's brother-in-law, stopped by to pick up some nails. The two men had a quiet discussion as they watched Rivetina drive away.

The following day, Rivetina stopped back at Mrs. Chen's to double-check on the new pipes and see that everything was holding up well. She then added the decorative stepping stones. As she was finishing, Mrs. Chen approached her with a gift.
"Hello, Tina; I would like to give you a little something for helping me out."
"Oh, no, Mrs. Chen. I couldn't take one of your wind chimes. I know how much you love those!" the helpful fairy exclaimed.

"Come, come now." Mrs. Chen gently scolded. "I have eight of these things hanging around this garden, and I would really like to give you one as a 'thank you.' Don't make me put your name on my board!" She giggled and handed over the musical treasure.

Rivetina clutched it tightly. "Thank you, Mrs. Chen. This is a lovely present." She waved her hand extravagantly over the lawn. "Mrs. Chen, consider your wish granted!"

Anthony and Amy Henderson came rushing into the yard and began tugging on Rivetina's arms. "Hurry, hurry!" they shouted. "We have something really important to show you!"
Rivetina laughed. "Oh, um ok. Wow, hold on you guys! My legs need to catch up with your minds!"

The children led Rivetina to the edge of town, where a small crowd had formed by the welcome sign. Mr. Wimble stepped forward and began to speak.

"Tina Smith, it has come to our attention that you have been helping people all over Hamilton, and we think that it is time we all did something nice for you. So, here is a little present that I hope will make your day."

He grinned and pulled the cloth off of a new sign that had just been put up. Rivetina cupped her hands over her mouth and smiled as wide as a whale's gulp. The town of Hamilton now had a sign introducing her to the rest of the world.

"Rivetina, the hardcore . . . wish granting fairy . . . consider your wish granted!"

Everyone cheered.

A Final Thought:

Kindness is never a form of currency; it is always a gift.

a.d.j.

a.d.j. (April Dawn Jones) is an artist who lives in the beautiful mountains of West Virginia. With an English degree from WVU in Morgantown, and an Animation degree from Regent University in Virginia Beach; she possesses a burning passion for storytelling in a wide variety of forms. Often finding deep inspiration in nature, and her quirky pet companions, April prefers to let stories grow themselves.

"The joy of Rivetina is the often simple, but significant ways in which people care for one another. Showing someone else that they matter to you, is one of the very best gifts that you can give."

www.ingramcontent.com/pod-product-compliance
Lightning Source LLC
Chambersburg PA
CBRC090957100726
47911CB00008B/180